Flight and Fancy

The Airline Industry

Library of Congress Cataloging-in-Publication Data

Murray, Jennifer.
    Flight and fancy : the airline industry / by Jennifer Murray.
       p. cm. -- (Shockwave)
    Includes index.
    ISBN-10: 0-531-17796-3 (lib. bdg.)
    ISBN-13: 978-0-531-17796-9 (lib. bdg.)
    ISBN-10: 0-531-15486-6 (pbk.)
    ISBN-13: 978-0-531-15486-1 (pbk.)
  1. Aeronautics--Juvenile literature. 2. Air travel--Juvenile literature
  I. Title. II. Series.

   TL547.M87 2007
   387.7--dc22

2007018963

Published in 2008 by Children's Press, an imprint of Scholastic Inc.,
557 Broadway, New York, New York 10012
www.scholastic.com

SCHOLASTIC, CHILDREN'S PRESS, and associated logos are trademarks
and/or registered trademarks of Scholastic Inc.

08 09 10 11 12 13 14 15 16 17
10 9 8 7 6 5 4 3 2 1

Printed in China through Colorcraft Ltd., Hong Kong

Author: Jennifer Murray
Educational Consultant: Ian Morrison
Editor: Jennifer Murray
Designer: Miguel Carvajal
Photo Researcher: Jamshed Mistry
Illustration by: Miguel Carvajal (pp. 20–21)

Photographs by: © Bernd Glasstetter (p. 5); **Getty Images** (A380 plane, cover; p. 3; pp. 8–9;
Charles Lindbergh, p. 13; 1920s passengers, p. 15; pp. 20–21; pp. 24–25; aircraft fumes, p. 31);
Ingram Image Library (Boeing, p. 31); **Jennifer and Brian Lupton** (teenagers, pp. 32–33);
Photolibrary (p. 7; p. 26; pp. 29–30); **Tranz: Corbis** (tennis, cover; Zeppelin airship, p. 11; airmail
plane, pp. 12–13; wing walker, p. 15; pp. 16–19; pp. 22–23; pp. 27–28; aircraft mechanic,
pp. 32–33); **Popperfoto** (*Hindenburg*, pp. 14–15); **Rex Features** (biplane, pp. 10–11).

The publisher would like to thank Captain Ian Murray for his expert advice.

All other illustrations and photographs © Weldon Owen Education Inc.

SHOCKWAVE
SOCIAL STUDIES

Flight and Fancy
The Airline Industry

Jennifer Murray

children's press®

An imprint of Scholastic Inc.
NEW YORK • TORONTO • LONDON • AUCKLAND • SYDNEY
MEXICO CITY • NEW DELHI • HONG KONG
DANBURY, CONNECTICUT

CHECK THESE OUT!

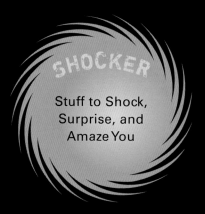

SHOCKER

Stuff to Shock,
Surprise, and
Amaze You

Quick Recaps
and Notable
Notes

Word Stunners
and Other Oddities

The Heads-Up
on Expert Reading

Links to More
Information

CONTENTS

aeronautical (*air uh NAW tik uhl*) to do with airplanes
and flying

aviation (*ay vee AY shuhn*) the science of building
and flying aircraft

circumnavigate (*sur kuhm NAV uh gayt*) to travel
all the way around something, such as flying
around the world

commercial (*kuh MUR shuhl*) to do with business
or making money

flammable (*FLAM uh buhl*) capable of catching fire
easily and burning quickly

fuselage (*FYOO suh lahj*) the main body of the
airplane that holds the crew, passengers, luggage,
and cargo

supersonic (*soo pur SAH nik*) faster than the speed
of sound

For additional vocabulary, see Glossary on page 34.

Circum in the word *circumnavigate*
is from the Latin meaning "around."
Related words include: *circumference*,
circus, *circumscribe*, and *circumstance*.

Airliner and crew in the 1950s

In 1929, an **aeronautical** engineer named Nevil Shute wrote about the future of air travel. Shute predicted that by 1980 the best **commercial** airplane ever built would have a top speed of 130 miles per hour and fly nonstop for 600 miles. How wrong he was!

The reality went far beyond the dreams of the early aircraft builders. By 1959, airplanes were carrying passengers nonstop across the Atlantic Ocean, a distance of 3,000 miles. In 1969, an airplane known as Concorde could reach a top speed of 1,490 miles per hour. In the same year, the Boeing 747 jumbo jet appeared. It could fly nonstop for 8,350 miles.

1914	1927	1932	1939
The St. Petersburg-Tampa Airboat Line company makes the world's first commercial airline flight in Florida.	American Charles Lindbergh becomes the first person to fly **solo** and nonstop across the Atlantic Ocean.	American Amelia Earhart becomes the first woman to fly solo and nonstop across the Atlantic Ocean.	The first **transatlantic** commercial flight, from New York to London, takes place. Fuel stops are made on the way.

Today, millions of people take flights all over the world. However, a century ago, things were very different. The early passengers were few, brave, and usually wealthy. Airplanes were noisy, uncomfortable, and often dangerous. The history of the airline industry is an exciting story.

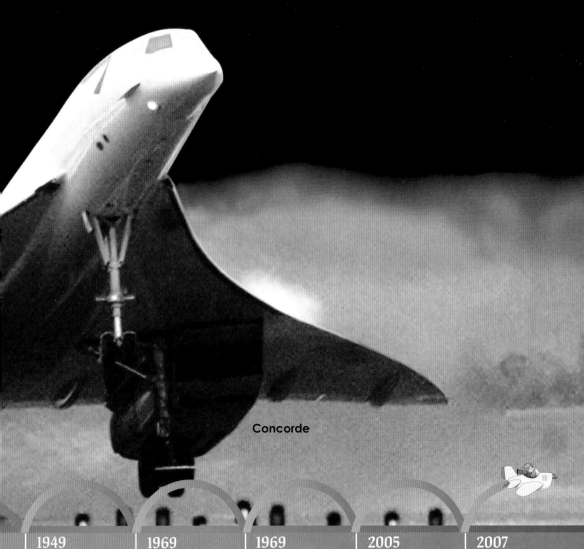

Concorde

1949

The first commercial airliner powered by jet engines, the de Havilland Comet, is flown for the first time in England.

1969

Boeing launches the 747, also called the Jumbo Jet.

1969

Supersonic passenger jet Concorde makes its test flight. Passenger service begins in 1976.

2005

Airbus tests the biggest passenger jet so far, the A380.

2007

Boeing launches a new, more fuel-efficient airliner, the 787.

9

The Early Days

In the early 1900s, flying was a new and dangerous business. Wilbur and Orville Wright had made the first powered flight in 1903. After that, **aviation** technology took off. Designers experimented with all kinds of flying machines. In the early days, **airships** were more popular than airplanes. Airships had been built since the mid-1800s. But, by 1909, despite the risks, a few brave passengers were taking to the skies in airplanes.

During World War I, airplanes became stronger and faster. When the war ended in 1918, there were suddenly surplus airplanes all over the United States and Europe. People realized that fighter planes and bombers could be converted and used to carry people or cargo. The airline industry had begun.

Initially, airlines grew faster in Europe than in the United States. Many railroad lines in Europe had been destroyed by war. The new airline services were able to become a major form of transportation. However, in the United States, the railroad service was good. It covered long distances. Even in 1918, it was comfortable and fast. The big challenge was to persuade the public to use a new and highly mistrusted method of travel.

Early Airline Industry

Paragraph 1	After 1903, aviation technology took off.
Paragraph 2	The airline industry began after World War I.
Paragraph 3	The airline industry grew much more quickly in Europe.

Airships were sometimes called zeppelins after the German airship designer Count Ferdinand von Zeppelin. Early airships were filled with **hydrogen**. Passenger and crew compartments hung underneath. In 1910, airships were flown regularly between cities in Germany. Soon afterwards, they flew all over Europe.

✂ Did You Know? ✂

On March 8, 1910, a French woman named Baroness Raymonde de Laroche became the first female licensed pilot.

Many early airplanes were **biplanes**. They had open **cockpits**. There was very little protection for the pilot and passenger. Extremely warm clothing was a must! The pilot sat in the rear seat, behind the passenger.

11

Airmail to Airlines

Airlines in the United States developed out of the airmail routes. Airplanes carried mail for the U.S. Postal Service. It was dangerous work to be a mail pilot. There were no maps, so pilots had to find their way by looking for landmarks. Many pilots got lost. Until 1923, they could not fly at night, because **airstrips** were not lit after dark.

Throughout the 1920s, very few passengers traveled by air. Most air transportation companies made their money through airmail deliveries. In 1927, there were only 30 airplanes in the U.S. that were capable of carrying passengers. Then, in May 1927, public interest in flying was aroused by the achievements of a former mail pilot named Charles Lindbergh.

The creation of the airline industry was responsible for the creation of many new words beginning with the prefix *air-*. On these two pages alone, there are five of them: *airmail*, *airlines*, *airstrips*, *airplanes*, and *airfield*.

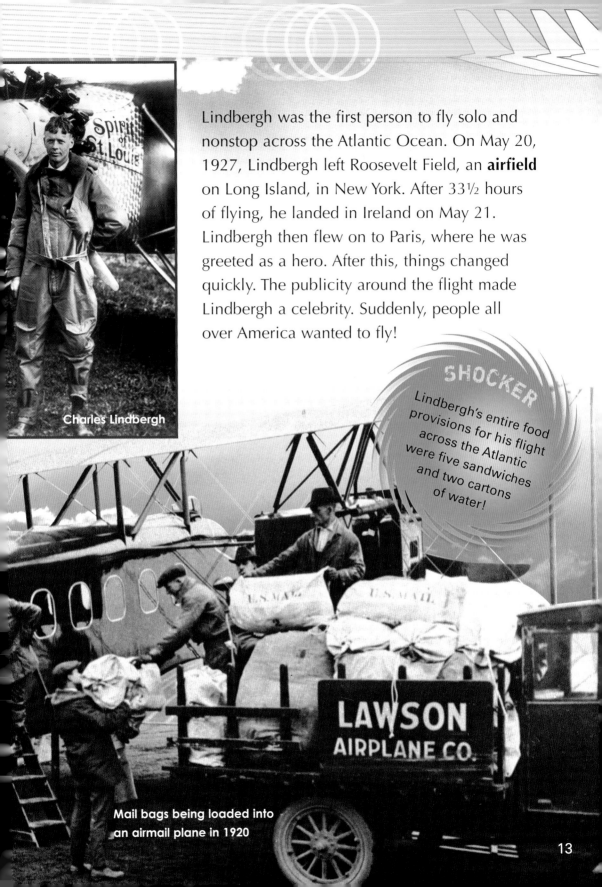

Lindbergh was the first person to fly solo and nonstop across the Atlantic Ocean. On May 20, 1927, Lindbergh left Roosevelt Field, an **airfield** on Long Island, in New York. After 33½ hours of flying, he landed in Ireland on May 21. Lindbergh then flew on to Paris, where he was greeted as a hero. After this, things changed quickly. The publicity around the flight made Lindbergh a celebrity. Suddenly, people all over America wanted to fly!

Charles Lindbergh

SHOCKER

Lindbergh's entire food provisions for his flight across the Atlantic were five sandwiches and two cartons of water!

LAWSON AIRPLANE CO.

Mail bags being loaded into an airmail plane in 1920

Tricks and Trips

The first successful passenger airplane made in the United States was the Ford Tri-Motor. It was built by a company owned by Henry Ford. Henry Ford was famous for starting the Ford Motor Company, which built automobiles. During World War I, Ford turned his attention to aviation. After the war, he continued to build **civilian** aircraft. The Ford Tri-Motor was made of **corrugated** metal. It was nicknamed the Tin Goose, and was first flown in 1926. It could carry 12 passengers, which was far more than any other plane at the time.

The U.S. company Transcontinental Air Transport (TAT) was one of the first airlines to make a profit from carrying passengers. In 1928, TAT got together with railroad companies to offer a coast-to-coast service across the U.S. It took passengers two days to get across the country, flying in Ford Tri-Motors during the day and taking railroad sleeper cars at night.

> The prefix *tri* in words such as Tri-Motor means "three." Similar words include: *triangle* (3 angles); *trimaran* (boat with 3 hulls); *trisect* (split into 3 parts).

Throughout the 1920s, airships continued to carry ▶ passengers. They even flew across the Atlantic. However, the hydrogen gas that filled the airship balloon was highly **flammable**. After several disasters in the 1930s, airships were rarely used as passenger aircraft. One of the worst disasters occurred in Lakehurst, New Jersey, on May 6, 1937. A German zeppelin, named the *Hindenburg*, caught fire while landing. Thirty-six people were killed.

The *Hindenburg* on fire

◀ **Wing walker**

During the 1920s, flying circuses and stunt flying were popular. The stunt pilots were known as **barnstormers**. They performed daring air shows. Sometimes wing walkers leaped from the wing of one plane to another mid-flight! There were terrible accidents, but the circuses fed the public enthusiasm for flying.

These wicker chairs may look stylish, but actually ▲ flying in the 1920s was uncomfortable. There was no soundproofing inside the cabin, so it was very noisy. There was also no heating.

The Age of Glamour

The 1930s were the age of glamour for air travel. Airplanes were getting bigger. They were able to carry more fuel, so they could fly farther. Airlines realized that passenger comfort was an important part of persuading people to fly. Improvements in soundproofing and **insulation** made the cabins more pleasant to travel in. However, only business people and the wealthy could afford to travel by air.

▲

Comfort was especially important on long-distance routes. Cabins were carpeted. During the 1930s, some planes even showed in-flight movies. Planes often had large windows so that passengers had a good view during the flight. However, before there were flight attendants, the passengers were the ones who served tea or coffee – to each other!

Passengers watching a movie

Even so, flying was not always glamorous! Early airline cabins were not supplied with oxygen for the passengers and crew. High in the sky, there was not enough oxygen to breathe, so airplanes had to fly below a certain **altitude**. During early high-altitude flights, passengers wore oxygen masks. The airplane could then cruise at 20,000 feet without causing the passengers discomfort. Today, cabins are **pressurized** and have plenty of oxygen so most airliners cruise at about 35,000 feet.

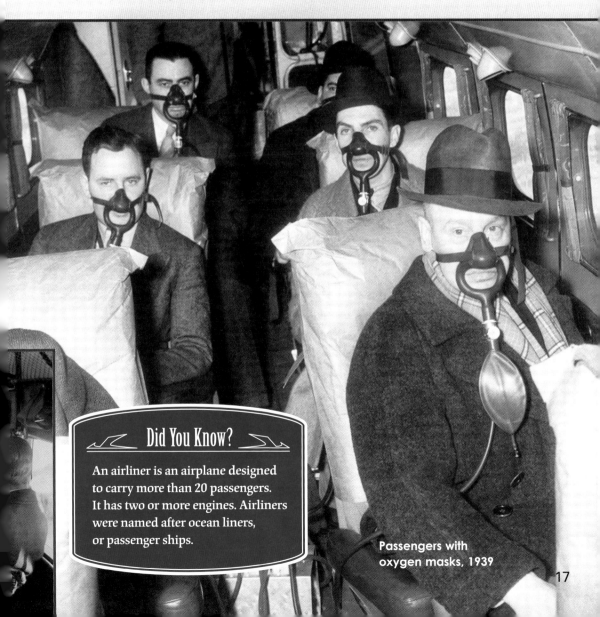

Did You Know?

An airliner is an airplane designed to carry more than 20 passengers. It has two or more engines. Airliners were named after ocean liners, or passenger ships.

Passengers with oxygen masks, 1939

By the mid-1930s, airplanes had started to resemble the airliners we know today. The DC-3 was one of these. It appeared in 1936 in two versions: a daytime model and a sleeper model. Passengers could travel in more comfort than ever before. The seats and bunks were upholstered and mounted on rubber, which reduced the vibrations that passengers felt during the flight. The DC-3 could also fly higher than previous airplanes. This meant that it could fly above the worst air **turbulence**. Turbulence made some passengers very scared and even sick, so this was a big improvement.

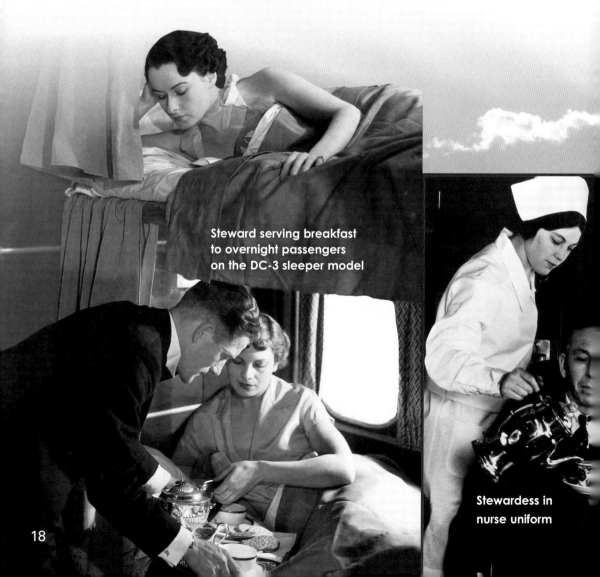

Steward serving breakfast to overnight passengers on the DC-3 sleeper model

Stewardess in nurse uniform

Some airlines had started to employ special crew to take care of passengers. To begin with, these attendants were all male. They were called air stewards. Stewards carried and loaded luggage, helped nervous passengers, and sometimes served drinks during the flight. In 1930, a nurse named Ellen Church persuaded Boeing Air Transport that women could do the job just as well as male stewards.

Air stewardess, 1935 ▶

SHOCKER

In 1990, flight attendant Nigel Ogden saved a pilot's life when a window broke in the flight deck while the plane was flying. The pilot was sucked halfway out of the window! Ogden grabbed the pilot's belt. He held on until the plane landed.

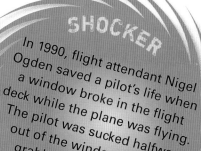

The first female flight attendants stepped on board Boeing Air Transport flights on May 15, 1930. They were called air stewardesses. Their job was to make passengers feel happier and more comfortable during the flight. Like stewards, stewardesses carried baggage, took tickets, tidied the cabin, and offered food and drinks during the flight. Sometimes they handed out chewing gum, which helped ease ear pain during takeoff or landing.

1920s	1930s
• uncomfortable chairs	• much more comfort
• self-service	• special service crew
• no heating	• better insulation

19

The Flying Boat

For many passengers in the 1930s, flying boats represented excitement, luxury travel, and exotic destinations. The **fuselage** of a flying boat was designed to act like the hull of a ship. This allowed the aircraft to land and float on water. The fuselage was **streamlined** so that the flying boat could reach the speed required to take off.

Flying boats were the first airliners to fly very long distances. Land-based airliners were limited in the distances that they could fly, because they needed airfields at which to stop and refuel. However, flying boats could stop at islands, on rivers or lakes, and along coasts to refuel and pick up supplies. By 1935, flying boats were carrying passengers to India, the Middle East, and even as far away as Australia and New Zealand. Some of these flights took several days, with many stops made on the way. At this time, very few flying boats were able to land on airfields as well as on water. These **amphibious** flying boats were developed later.

I found that as I was reading I was drawn to looking at the illustrations. These are really useful in helping me understand how flying boats worked.

Inside the Boeing 314 Flying Boat

KEY

1. Deluxe suite
2. Bathrooms
3. Baggage compartments
4. Seating
5. Sleeping berths
6. Dining room/lounge
7. Wing walkway for mechanics
8. Navigator's chart room
9. Flight deck
10. Crew room

Did You Know?

In January 1943, Franklin Roosevelt became the first serving U.S. president to travel in a plane. He flew in a Boeing 314 to Casablanca, North Africa.

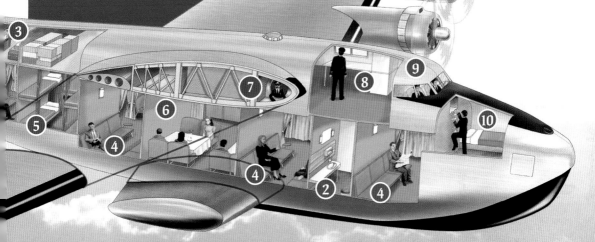

The Boeing 314 was a gigantic flying boat. It was nicknamed the Clipper, after the great oceangoing sailing ships of the nineteenth century. It was built by Boeing, which was one of the major aviation manufacturers. The Clipper could fly from London to New York in 23 hours. Inside, it had everything passengers might need for a comfortable flight.

21

War and a New Start

During World War II, airlines used their planes to help in the war effort. Trans World Airlines (TWA) volunteered its planes to carry troops and equipment for the United States military. Developments in flying during this time were focused mainly on military airplanes, such as fighters. Advances included pressurized cabins, which allowed airplanes to fly at high altitudes without the pilots or passengers needing oxygen masks.

SHOCKER

On June 1, 1943, the Germans shot down a DC-3 passenger airplane. They wanted to **assassinate** the British Prime Minister, Winston Churchill, who they thought was on the plane. Everyone was killed. Churchill was not on board.

The demand for airplanes during the war meant that new airplanes had to be produced quickly. This led to a shortage of materials. The public were asked to donate any scrap metal, such as old pans, metal gates, or fences. The scrap metal was melted down and used to build new airplanes.

Women finishing propellers made in an aircraft factory during World War II

After World War II, progress in aviation was slower in Europe than in the United States. Many of Europe's factories and airstrips had been destroyed by bombing. The U.S. had not been affected in this way. Advances in aviation technology made during the war years were used in the building of commercial passenger airplanes.

Now that's interesting! I found myself turning back to see what happened to aviation at the end of World War I. Back then, Europe was well ahead of America, which was just the opposite. I'm glad I went back and checked.

◄ The Boeing Stratocruiser was the 1948 passenger-carrying version of a bomber flown during World War II. The Stratocruiser was modified yet again by NASA in 1965. NASA used the new version to transport huge spacecraft parts for the space program. The front section of the plane opened completely to accommodate huge cargo. This strange-looking airplane was named Guppy, because it looked like the fish of that name.

23

The Jet Age

Triumph and Tragedy

During the 1940s, an English aeronautical designer named Frank Whittle developed a **turbine** engine. This became known as the jet engine. The jet engine would replace propeller-driven engines, and lead to faster, higher flight. The change to jet airliners took more than a decade. The United States had large, comfortable, and reliable propeller-driven airliners, such as the DC-3, which airlines were reluctant to abandon. Progress toward jet travel was also slowed by the tragic events in the development of the sleek, elegant airplane named the Comet.

For 31 minutes on July 27, 1949, the design team of British aircraft company de Havilland watched the Comet **prototype** fly for the first time. This flight was the result of three years' hard work. Another three years of test-flying, training, and inspections would take place before the Comet took to the air as the world's first commercial jet airliner. The jet age had begun!

Did You Know?

The Comet prototype was flown by John Cunningham, a World War II pilot and de Havilland's chief test pilot. During the war, he was known as Cat's Eyes Cunningham, because of his ability to see in the dark. Actually, this was because he was one of the first pilots to use **radar** to navigate at night.

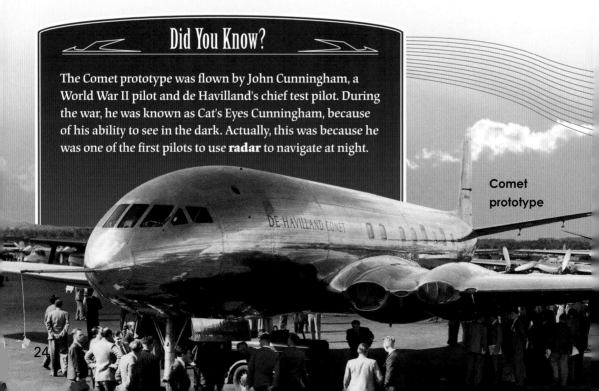

DE HAVILLAND COMET

Comet prototype

Then, in 1952, disaster struck. A Comet leaving Rome crashed. Luckily, nobody was killed. In 1953, a Comet crashed as it took off from Pakistan, killing everyone on board. Another exploded over India during bad weather. In 1954, a Comet exploded in the air over Italy. An investigation began. At first, the investigators decided that Comets could keep flying. Their decision was reversed later in 1954, when yet another Comet crashed on its way to Egypt. The wreckage found in the ocean suggested that it too had exploded.

Accident Investigation

The Comet Tragedies

The investigation concluded that, flying at speeds of 500 miles an hour and at an altitude of about 30,000 feet, the new Comet jet airliner was subjected to greater pressure than any airliner ever before. The result was metal fatigue, which caused the metal structures to crack and fall apart. The investigation found cracks in the fuselage. The cracks had started at the edge of the square windows. The fatal flaw seemed to be the window design. The square shape could not withstand the forces of jet flight. Ever since the investigation into the Comet disasters, jet airplanes have had rounded instead of square-cornered windows.

◄ Fuselage wreckage under examination

Causes
- speed exceeding 500 mph
- altitude exceeding 30,000 feet
- square window design

Effects
- extreme pressure buildup
- metal fatigue
- cracks at windows

Onward and Upward

Throughout the 1950s, British aviation struggled under the cloud of the Comet disasters. Meanwhile, airline industries around the world were busy catching up with the demand for jet travel. In the U.S., Boeing was working on the 707 prototype. The 707 became the first commercially successful jet airliner. However, during the late 1950s and the 1960s, the number of passengers increased rapidly. Eventually, the 707 was too small to cope with the demand. Boeing went on to develop seven more models, starting with the 727 in 1963.

As the number of flights increased, airports also had to be developed quickly. Airports needed runways, catering facilities, baggage-handling facilities, and ticket services. Air-traffic control also improved. It was important to avoid crashes and to prevent airlines from interfering with military flying. Air-traffic controllers used radar, radios, signal lights, and other equipment to direct planes on the ground and in the air.

Air-traffic controllers often work in a tower located high above the airport.

The air-traffic control tower is the center of operations at the airport. Air-traffic controllers work around the clock to monitor arriving and departing flights.

SHOCKER

In 1958, more transatlantic passengers traveled by air than by sea for the first time.

The engines on the 1963 Boeing 727 were attached to the rear of the fuselage, instead of under the wing as on other Boeing airliners. This sometimes made the 727 more turbulent, but it also made the passenger cabin very quiet. The 727 was sometimes called the Whisperjet because passengers could speak to each other in a whisper and still be heard. Before the 727 was built, whispering to someone while flying in a jet plane was impossible!

Boeing 727

Did You Know?

In the 1960s and 1970s, nearly all airlines had a policy that flight attendants must be between 5'2" and 6' in height. This was so that attendants could reach the overhead lockers easily and were not too tall for the sometimes cramped cabins. At that time, several airlines also stated that only unmarried women could be flight attendants!

Bigger and Better

In 1969, jumbo jet service began when Boeing launched a new, massive project. Originally, the term *jumbo jet* meant any large or wide airplane, but it has come to mean one particular airliner – the Boeing 747. The 747 was based on an unbuilt military design. With four huge jet engines, it had a range of 8,350 miles, a maximum speed of 604 miles per hour, and seating for more than 400 passengers.

The size of the 747 added new luxuries to air travel. The design included an upper deck, where the flight deck and a first-class lounge were situated. Recent models have included bunk beds for passengers to sleep in. There have even been plans to add a gym. In 2005, the European company Airbus built a rival airliner. The huge A380 has been named Superjumbo. It carries up to 555 passengers.

Did You Know?

Howard Hughes was an American businessman, movie producer, and **aviator**. In the 1940s, he designed the largest plane ever built. It was a huge, wooden flying boat, nicknamed Spruce Goose. It had a **wingspan** of 319 feet, 11 inches. It had eight engines and room for 700 passengers. However, it flew only once, in 1947, with Hughes at the controls.

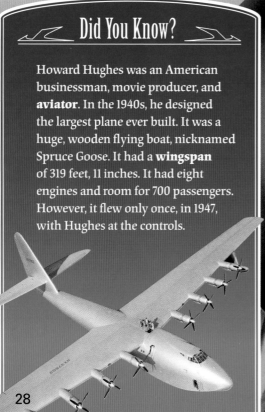

Mechanic servicing a jet engine

Boeing 767 flight deck

There are usually two pilots flying a commercial airplane. They are the captain and the copilot. They fly the plane from the flight deck. Instrument panels monitor the engines and the progress of the flight. The instruments also provide the pilots with information to keep the airplane on course.

SHOCKER

On May 24, 1991, a jumbo airlifted a record-breaking 1,087 passengers out of Ethiopia. The passenger count became 1,088 when a baby was born during the flight!

Increase in Size and Capacity

27 feet

1919   Curtiss Jenny
4 passengers

92 feet

1928   Handley Page HP 42
38 passengers

106 feet

1935   Boeing 314 Flying Boat
74 passengers

1969   Boeing 747-100
374–490 passengers

231 feet

2005   Airbus A380 Superjumbo
555 passengers

239 feet

Fast but Flawed

In 1947, military jet airplanes had flown faster than the speed of sound. However, it was not until 1969 that the supersonic airliner named Concorde flew for the first time. Concorde is still the only supersonic airliner to have carried passengers on a regularly scheduled service.

Initially, 70 orders were received for Concorde from airlines around the world, but several events led to the cancellation of most of these orders. Conflict in the Middle East resulted in the oil crisis of 1973. This limited the fuel available to the United States, western Europe, and Japan. As Concorde used far more fuel than **subsonic** airliners, many airlines felt it was financially impossible to run a supersonic service. The crash of a rival Russian prototype also raised questions about the safety of supersonic jet travel.

SHOCKER

Concorde held many records, including that of **circumnavigating** the world nonstop in 31 hours, 27 minutes, and 49 seconds in August 1995.

I remember seeing pictures of the Concorde. It has a strange nose that seems to point down. It's great being able to make these sorts of connections. It makes reading easier, and a lot more fun.

Another problem was the **environmental** concern about the noise made by Concorde. The sonic boom is a huge noise created at the point the airplane passes the speed of sound. Many people objected to the noise. This led the U.S. to cancel its own supersonic program in 1971. Countries such as India and Malaysia refused to allow Concorde to land, or even fly over their air space. In the end, only Air France and British Airways operated Concorde services. Concorde flew regularly between Europe and the U.S. The service began on January 21, 1976 and ended completely on October 24, 2003.

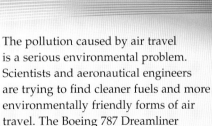

Boeing 787

The pollution caused by air travel is a serious environmental problem. Scientists and aeronautical engineers are trying to find cleaner fuels and more environmentally friendly forms of air travel. The Boeing 787 Dreamliner is the latest step toward these goals. The 787 is made of **carbon fiber**. This is much lighter than aluminum, which most aircraft are made of. The 787 also has curved wings, which cause less **drag**. These design **innovations** reduce the amount of fuel needed to fly the 787.

Not everyone is sure that traveling by air is safe. There have been accidents caused by mechanical problems. However, these are rare. Many checks are done on airliners to make sure that they are in top condition. Some people worry that the risks of sabotage are very high. **Terrorist** threats and attacks in the last few years have frightened some passengers. They think that airliners need even more security, perhaps having security guards on all flights.

WHAT DO YOU THINK?

Do you think that flying in airliners is safe?

PRO

Flying is very safe. There are so many precautions. When you go through the airport, everything you have with you is searched. There are many accidents on the road each year, but we still travel in cars. I would take a flight without any worries.

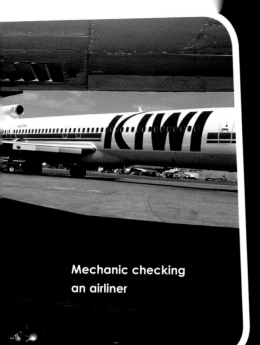

Mechanic checking an airliner

However, there are strict checks on the passengers and baggage boarding airliners. X-ray scanners make sure nothing dangerous is taken onto airplanes. According to **statistics**, flying is the safest form of transportation. There are accidents in cars every day. There are far more boat and train accidents than airliner crashes. More than three million people fly safely on commercial airliners every day.

CON

Flying is dangerous. If something does go wrong you are a long way above the ground, and you will probably die. Also, however strict security checks are, they may not be enough. I think people should be more wary of flying.

GLOSSARY

Biplane

airfield a landing ground with fuel supplies for airplanes

airship a power-driven aircraft kept in the air by a body of gas

airstrip a landing ground used by airplanes

altitude (*AL ti tood*) the height of something above the ground

amphibious (*am FIB ee uhss*) water and land based, such as an airplane designed to land on both water and land

assassinate to murder someone who is well known or important

aviator a pilot

barnstormer a stunt pilot

biplane an airplane with two sets of wings, one mounted above the other

carbon fiber a strong, lightweight, humanmade material

civilian non-military

cockpit the area in a plane where the pilot sits

corrugated (*KOR oh gay tid*) shaped into ridges or ripples

drag the force that acts on something to slow it down

environmental to do with the area or surrounding natural habitat

hydrogen (*HYE druh juhn*) a gas that is highly flammable

innovation something that has not been tried before, or an improvement to an existing invention

insulation a lining or cover that stops heat from escaping

pressurized maintaining a near normal pressure and oxygen supply during high-altitude flight

prototype the first version of a new invention or design

radar (*RAY dar*) a device that locates objects by reflecting radio waves off them and receiving the reflected waves

solo alone

statistic a fact expressed as a number

streamlined designed to move through air or water quickly and easily

subsonic less than the speed of sound

terrorist relating to an illegal military group

transatlantic to do with crossing the Atlantic Ocean

turbine an engine driven by gas passing through the blades of a wheel and making it revolve

turbulence bumpiness caused by disturbed air currents

wingspan the distance across the wings of an airplane, from tip to tip

FIND OUT MORE

BOOKS

Dartford, Mark. *Fighter Planes*. Lerner Publishing Company, 2003.

Herbst, Judith. *The History of Transportation*. Twenty-First Century Books, 2005.

Masters, Nancy Robinson. *The Airplane*. Franklin Watts, 2004.

Rees, Peter. *How Does It Fly?: The Science of Flight*. Scholastic Inc., 2008.

Rinard, Judith E. *Book of Flight: The Smithsonian National Air and Space Museum*. Firefly Books, 2007.

WEB SITES

Go to the Web sites below to learn more about the airline industry.

www.nasm.si.edu/exhibitions/gal100/index.cfm

www.century-of-flight.freeola.com

www.spartacus.schoolnet.co.uk/Aviation.htm

http://library.thinkquest.org/3785

INDEX

ABOUT THE AUTHOR

Jennifer Murray loves to travel by air; she thinks taking off in an airplane is very exciting. As a child, Jennifer visited many air shows with her father, who was a pilot. He used to point out the different airplanes and tell her about the history of flight. Sometimes she was even allowed to sit in the flight deck when her father was flying!